HAMSTER, RATS & OTHER STUFF GOING ON …

Nitsa Anastasiades

To Soulla, Elly, George and Tassos:
all journeys begin with a single step.

CONTENTS

OPPORTUNITY KNOCKS

For as long as I can remember, we've had to help Dad at
the chip shop on Friday nights.

One Friday, when I was ironing still, upstairs at our house
in Twickenham, I looked out the window. At eighteen,
you notice certain things, like Tyra over the road
being picked up by her boyfriend again; every night, in
fact, those past two weeks: the same Cavalier— white,
smooth, second hand— his arm on the wheel and a smirk
peering up at me as if to say: 'Youwish it were *you* in this
car, don't you?'

I did

It was the usual nuts Friday: chips chucked in and out of
sizzling baskets faster than you could say, 'saveloy'.
Takings were high again, too: six hundred in six
hours. Back in '82, that was a neat little bundle to stick in
your brown leather case at the back of your kitchen
cupboard ready to bank Monday mornings.

When we got back to the house, though, none of us
noticed at first. Dad had gone to the kitchen, as usual,
Mum, the loo. It was my sister, Katie, who shouted,
then my brother, Ted.

'Hey! My clothes have been chucked about.'

'What? My record player's missing.'

Dad couldn't move from the kitchen table. 'Fifteen thousand,' he kept saying, hands in his precious case.

'Ready to bank at Barclays that was—'

'Don't get me started on *that* again,' Mum said.

A month later, when I was cutting into the nape of a regular's hair at Loretta's Salon in Winchmore Hill where I was training, she told me, blank cold, that her son was going to prison.

'What??' I said, 'Why?'

An exclusive road in Longmore Park, she said. Spent all the cash in three days on jewellery, video machines and cars, two of which were Vauxhall, the Cavalier types? — his favourite.

PAULINA & ME

We were mad, we were crazy, Paulina and me—running
through parks, our feet grazing the daises, arms stretched
out wide—
'You!'
'No, you.'
'No, *you* go!'
And we'd tease each other to see if he'd do it—the man
in the mac—his quick flash. But we didn't; wouldn't dare
… only Jess, the one who looked after her gran in the
chair, the girl who said nothing at school, the one who
smelled like rats, cats, Paulina & me—we told her to
meet Roy Jenkins in the park at night. She got all dressed
up for the occasion. Told her gran she'd be in by eleven.
Raging down Soho at weekends, throwing our heads in
sex shops, asking how much— *pleeeease?* —for a quick
peep. I'll pay *you*, said the man, pointing at Paulina, to
do it right there, on the stage, over there—yah, *na – ked*—
picking his teeth.
Tut.
Put a teaspoon down our pants, Paulina, me; watched the
puffed-up lady stir her tea— pinched each other's skin so
we wouldn't scream, till she quaffed it all down …

Dying each other's hair black, matt, fluorescent tips,
pink—sticking earrings down our cheeks, lips, tits,
jumping on tubes, roofs, smoking spliffs—
'Miss Lusby. Miss Lusby! You got a boyfriend, Miss
Lusby? Miss Lusby?? Where d'you get your shoes, Miss
Lusby? Does your boyfriend have a sexy bum, Miss
Lusby? *Ooooh* la la! You said the 'f' word, I'm telling
the head, Ms Lusby.'
Then, we'd run out of class … chucked our books over
the wall come exam time, hoisted our butts on the back of
Roy's bike—me hugging Paulina's bump tight—the wind
soaring, our eyes stinging; tears oozing for the memory of
Jess, bless, best friends— and all the damned silly stupid
things we still hadn't done yet together.

MELANIE

The best thing about my job back then was the people
you met, their stories … how they'd confide in you. I
remember this one time, in October, I think it was—a
typical English afternoon: freezing. I'd finished work
early, was tired; didn't want to go out again, when a lady
named Melanie called, said she'd pay me double if I'd
go. I thought it a bit odd, then: 'I'm desperate to sort out
my hair,' she said. 'I've been in hospital for a long time
and am nervous about letting anyone near it.' The person
coming had to be gentle, understanding, patient, as you
lose your confidence in a situation like that. I
immediately thought the worst and a pain twinged at my
heart, so I booked her. 'Please don't be surprised when
you see me,' she added. I'll write what I remember.

Number twenty-three flashed momentarily through my
wipers as I turned into Hygrove Close. I parked neatly
outside Melanie's house.
The rain, well drizzle, came down a touch heavier, so I
grabbed my case and made my way, hoodie up, through
her gate to the front porch. Marigolds, chrysanthemums:
all colours, in neat rows, bobbed in syncopation in the

front garden, and a lace curtain from the bay window downstairs slid back to its original position.

'Hello, Sally.' A tall, wide figure stood before me. Six foot four? She wore a tartan skirt to her ankles, a pair of low cream heels, and a matching long sleeved blouse with a tie at the neck. Her hair was bobbed, shoulder length, a chocolaty shade—the fringe too long for her false, curled lashes.

'I'm Melanie.'

She held out her hand and smiled briefly, the shadowed skin wrinkling, then softening beneath her eyes. Her handshake was weak and slipped out of mine. 'Please, come in.'

The hallway smelled of pine. There was a woman at the top of the stairs hoovering.

'This is my mother,' Melanie gestured, walking ahead, and Mother—a full busted lady in her mid-sixties with a round body and a bright pink face—waved enthusiastically from above. Melanie squeezed out the loud din of the hoover as I followed her into the kitchen, where she shut the door behind us.

'I'll get straight to the point,' she said with renewed confidence. 'I've been in hospital for a long time, as I told you and …' she hesitated, 'I'm a transsexual.'

Her wig, I realized, was cheap; a disappointment seeing the quality of the house: white wood units bending smoothly around corners, stainless steel fixtures, and an impressive black granite bar as the centerpiece, topped with white lilies.

She led me to a floral papered room, where, sitting there, I wondered why I felt suddenly … betrayed, was it? — whether this was selfish of me, and, well …why didn't she just first tell me?

She called me back to the kitchen where she'd put a chair on some plastic sheeting and a full-sized mirror opposite, against the bar.

Melanie explained the shape of the haircut: 'Not asymmetric, you understand—just straight across, but not obviously so. I don't want to have that just-cut-look, if you know what I mean.'

I returned my Jowel's to their leather case, reluctantly, and took out my cheaper scissors I used often for lopping off larger amounts. This 'hair' tugged against the comb, I— against the knots; there was no way I was going to use my two hundred quid babies on this rubbish. Even training on mannequins at John Frieda had been a synthetic and pure mix.

'It's OK to cut with it on, yes?'

No, actually.

'Um, we'll give it a go,' I said. 'It'll be fine.'

Luckily, the wig was a tight fit, so hardly moved at all. In any case, I hadn't brought enough crocodile clips to secure it down, and when it did slip, Melanie helped by holding on to the front as I trimmed off the three quarters of an inch she kept insisting on.

Keep your head still.

I moved to the front to chip into the fringe. Texturise here a little—a slight arch effect between the brows—check the lengths on either side, and yep, I'd be out of there.

'It's not a bad one, is it? I got it from Harvey Nichols; was quite expensive. It looks natural, don't you think? Especially now you've cut it.'

To my surprise, Melanie yanked off the wig. Underneath, a gleaming head presented itself: bare, but for a few pockets of dark grey frizzled bits above the ears and in the crinkled nape of the neck: an old man's neck.

'You don't mind, do you? Just cut it right back, will you? It gets terribly itchy otherwise.'

I just stood there, and all I could hear was my father's voice: *'You put yourself at risk going mobile. You never know what loony you might meet, going into their houses. Why you didn't take on that salon partnership ...'* Lost, Dad, *lost* my share after my boyfriend, Matt, ran away with it all.

'You do have clippers?' Melanie asked.

Yeees, I take all my equipment with me.

I slid the number one attachment onto the clippers, turned on the motor and buzzed away.

'I battled for years, you know. Was married. Have three kids. But I just woke up one morning, I did, and I said to myself: No more, Terry, I said, no more. Now it's my time to be *me*.'

She reached under the cape and showed me a photo from her pocket. Three blonde boys: one on each knee, the tallest about my little brother Danny's age, back then— 11? —standing behind him, grinning, resting his chin on a very handsome young Terry's head. They shared almost identical hair.

'I know,' Melanie said, reading my mind. 'Amazing, wasn't it? So thick, *and* curly, back then. Lost it with all the stress.' She tutted.

I looked around for a picture of her wife, their mother … 'We're on slightly better terms now, of course, thank the Lord.' She raised her voice over the droning. 'It's taking a while though, Sally: baby steps … and I go up and down, you know? The hospital's been wonderful getting me to see a psychologist for three months, who's really helped me, especially with all the initial family goings on. Hey!' she jumped up. 'Do you like Fashion TV? It's on about now.'

Melanie's lipstick, a blood, now, looking red, with the wig off, had smudged down the right lower corner of her mouth, giving her, I thought, a slightly freakish look as she spun with my black cape, her ET-like shaped head (I'd watched the film earlier that week), flashing left, right, as she excitedly turned on the suspended TV. I recalled Matt then, how he'd ask me to recite to him my clients' stories at night, snuggled close. He'd usually wrap up each with some philosophical phrase, like: *Well, she's obviously lonely.* 'And now it's your turn,' I'd nudge, before he was completely out. 'Nothing to report today, I'm afraid, from Matthew's garage …' (where he was doing his barbering).

Mother came in—pink beaming face unchanged—and made for us all, tea: cinnamon hibiscus, she said, soothing.

'Here we are,' she winked at me, bringing over a tray with two white china cups and a matching teapot.

'Everything's always better with hot tea.'

Melanie joined; sat opposite me, at the kitchen bar. Her mum asked me about my family, how long I'd been in the area, whether I had kids, when I began going mobile? And didn't I prefer salon work, really? A boyfriend …? It was nice, honestly, having someone show genuine interest for a change, and I replied succinctly, remembering my training.

Melanie remained quiet throughout—her mother poured tea—viewing models prancing up, down the catwalk in figure hugging Versace dresses from her 2003 collection that year, some with slits up the front, others in leather, tassels hanging.

'You know,' Melanie said, both of us sipping. 'I was a correspondent for the News of the World. A renowned journalist for eighteen years.' Her spider lashes flashed, then lowered. I wished then she'd ask me to put back on the wig for her.

'A cutthroat world … oh, the stories I could tell you, Sally. They *shunned* me. And I was *good.* You remember the death of Princess Diana?'

'Yes.' She was my idol! I'd watched her wedding, had a day off school for it. I'd sat up in bed, full of cold, wishing Mum was around.

'Mmh,' Melanie swallowed, carefully placing down her cup with her large, manicured hands. 'I was supposed to cover that story. I had the main lead.'

'Really?'

Mother was making noises in the biscuit tin.

'Yes. I'd already gone over to Paris to the Pont de l'Alma. It was chaos, everyone doing anything to get whatever they could off her; the lengths they'd go to. And I was poisoned, Sally, the night before her crash occurred. Can you believe it? —*poisoned.'* She shook her head, then tilted it to the side. 'I was lucky my good friend Hugh was with me, or I mightn't have made it back. Tragic tale, still, whichever way we look at it, in the end for her, poor girl, so sad … when all she ever wanted was to live. We could have *saved* her.' Melanie inhaled. 'It's true what they say, though, you know, Sally: you should never believe what you read in the papers.'

I imagined Diana's body rising from that hospital table, flowering into swan's wings, joining my mother in heaven for tea.

And Melanie's mum's floral scent, then, mixed with her sweat as she leaned over to place down a plate of Hobnobs between us, smelled, strangely, comforting.

'How do you think she got that look, Sally?' Melanie regarded me with faded blue eyes. 'Diana, I mean?'

'Oh, a root-lift perm, definitely, and highlights—foil— not the cap.'

'… poised, yet so real?'

Mother exhaled noisily, then exited the kitchen with a mug and the biscuit tin.

'I … I guess it comes from …' I said, nervously, reaching for a Hobnob, *'within?'*

'She never had a big bust either, did she, Sally?'

I shot up my hand to my 32a sized chest, then understood she was talking about her own.

'Of course, I'm still taking hormones. They're really good with me at that hospital. And I only had to wait three years for the operation, which isn't bad for the

National Health, is it? Oh, wow! See? I just *love* that design …'

I glanced at my watch. The hour I'd booked for Melanie was almost up. I began packing away my things as she fumbled in her bag, apologizing, and calling out to her mother for more cash. We discussed highlights, then: red, to make her eyes pop more, and to bring out the tone in her skin. She was looking forward, as well, yes, she said, to going out into the world again, confidently, with this fabulous new look I was going to give her, and maybe contacting Hugh.

Two days before her appointment, however, Melanie called—left a message—her voice barely audible. Complications, she said; she'd caught some infection. I moved away from London not long after that—to Hertford, went back to uni; I'd been thinking about it for some time. I studied psychology, specialized in eating disorders, body image and families dealing with cancer. Any earlier misconceptions I'd had about Melanie's scheming to get me to her home that day, or regrets since, as to why I hadn't asked more about her work in-depth, or her family, or thanked her mother for caring, soon dissipated … I was in a different place, maybe, then, and young … plus, our Cosmetology training had taught us to: *Never discuss politics, religion, or anyone's love life.*

Yet, it's funny, still, how we connect, sometimes—
others' stories becoming our own, and so it goes on—
Like when I took my brother, Danny, with me to set a
lady's hair at the elderly flats once in Whickham. He
ended up going back to interview her on a bombing near
The Palladium during World War II, for his project. Her
friends had arranged a blind date for her and another girl,
apparently, with boys they both fell for. She was late, this
client, getting ready, and, by the time she got to the dance
hall, her friends, already inside, were killed. She was the
only survivor. My brother is now a ghost writer.
I thought about Melanie a few times during my study
years, and hope today she's found happiness, acceptance,
love, and lives a fulfilled life.

CONFESSION

You were down in the chip shop when I entered your room, your bedside cabinet I slowly opened. And there, deep inside, under the mangled hairbrush you never clean, in a box, lay your perfect necklace: a jewel in a casket.

You can't blame me. You never wore it. Only once I saw you, at Auntie Abel's baby's christening, and that was for show, not because you really liked it.

And now it's mine. And this time, I'm going to give it to Jenny, who'll wear it to art class when she makes diamond shapes on her clay pot with the Stanley knife she took from Mrs Martin's drawer before putting it in the clay oven to bake, so that it will last forever, and people will say, 'Hey. Remember the day Jenny wore that necklace on her birthday? Remember that day?'

THAT DATE WITH THE BOY AT THE TAPAS RESTAURANT

You know, I did go out with a boy once—when I was
sixteen and had just gotten a job at the local post
office. He came in and asked me for a date. I'd seen
him in the WH Smith's bookshop aisle where I used to go
into during my lunch hour, or after work sometimes.
I said, 'Yes' to him
straight away and joined him for lunch over the road at a
deserted tapas bar. He was small, wore black glasses and
his teeth were crooked with yellowish bits of what looked
like yesterday's Home Pride bread cheese sandwiches
stuck between them. But I said, '*Yes.*'
We ordered oval toasties with
mushroom, tomato oregano-olive topping, I think,
because each time he crunched, he scrunched up his nose
at me as if waiting for an answer. His hair, dark and
tousled (which I liked), was oily and dandruffed (I did
not like), all over the shoulders of his suit.
I don't really recall his voice, or what we spoke about
exactly (if at all), or why the tapas bar was so deserted. It
could have been because it was newly opened (I'd seen
lots of 'trendy' places advertised in our area, Ilford, in the

early eighties: wine bars, underground little 'nightclubs'
and suchlike), or perhaps we'd just gone on a late
sitting. I know my boss (Frances, back then), was never
keen on me leaving during the post office's rush hour.
He might have told me my eyes were nice (Father was
always saying: 'Deborah—you have nice eyes), or that
my hair was lovely (Father would tell
me it was this *strawberry* blonde, not that 'fire' red my
mother's had been when he first 'lured' her up north),
and I guess mine *was* wavy and longer back then.
Or maybe it was my plump milk skin that attracted him to
me (I have curved hips, small breasts and my legs are on
the thick side— too short for a dancer's still, but never
mind).
Now the other boy—well man, really (probably 21), at
the swimming baths—now *that* was a different matter.
He was the kind you knew you could never catch;
curly curly black hair, eyelashes, hazel, that looked
permanently wet around his pool topaz eyes, I'm telling
you. I used to go there a lot after work at one time, sit
mainly on the side and watch him train the swimmers up,
down. 'Now *that's* what I'm saying!'—his voice would
boom around the dripping walls, 'Elegance!
Everybody, look at Sharon.' And he'd start Sharon off
with the long, slow motions of his arms rising, brushing
past his ears behind him. And all the while he'd be

focusing on Sharon's rising bosom, oozing out the top of
her swimsuit. He looked up at me once, just as he did that
—so serious—like he was about to *say* something. I stood
up and ran out the baths so fast I never went back
there again, actually. Silly Sharon (he was tall—
6 foot 2 ish? —nice wide shoulders, long legs, and in
proportion. I'm five-foot three-quarter inches, but that
shouldn't matter?).

It could have been his dark hair. Yes. Or perhaps WH
Smith has some significance. I recall him looking at me
intently through his glasses, sideways, as I opened the
pages of Carmella Gertrude's *Fledglings in the
Basement.* It appealed to me enormously, that book,
because: here you have a girl—fourteen? Beautiful and
blonde. Her brother's a year older, also blonde and
wonderful, with a fringe too long flopping all over his
eyes. She's a gymnast—he wants to be a lawyer. Their
mother's a cow—locks them down in the basement.
Why? Because she's left their father (now why should
that be such a bad thing? —especially if a man is horrible
to you, ab*u*ses you, or something … why should you
stay, if you can get away?). Anyway, *she* did all this so
she could inherit her father's fortune estates or something
(and not end up as a shop assistant, because that's all she
knew), and her father didn't want her to marry that man
in the first place, plus he didn't know she had these kids,

so she was keeping them secret from him to get all that money.

My father always told me no one ever hands you anything on a plate for nothing. Ain't no shame in what you do, either, once you have it. Be a rubbish collector with a long sack and a pitchfork in the street, keep your head down, and damned well be that best long bag pitchfork rubbish collector that street has ever seen.

No such thing as a free lunch either, he still tells me, even after all this time. Be *wary*. You've always got to have the upper hand.

But I'd not been on *dates* (I suppose a husky telephone conversation with a boy from school for thirty seconds or so doesn't count), but *Fledglings in the Basement* was such a fulfilling read. My mother thought I had a bowel problem, because as soon as I got in from work, she'd want me to sit at the table straight away (Father took retirement early from carpentry because of an accident, losing his leg: *Bloody Foreigner*, a co-worker yelling, freeing him from the machinery) and not go upstairs to change or anything, where I might linger (or more likely tear open the pages of this book to get another look at its next instalment), and not do the washing up, or sit with Father and read to him, so she could finally escape, go into town again and do her 'other' things. So, I'd gobble down my food, be as polite as I could to my father, say, 'One minute,' then go straight up to the toilet and lock myself in. By goodness those were my best times.

Mary, the gymnast girl, who was going through puberty—getting boobs and everything— was practising her daily gymnastics moves down in the cellar and her brother noticed her. Well, you can imagine what happened next.

I don't think I could properly *fancy* my brother (even though I only have a younger one, and he left us too, years ago now). I always thought my cousin Andrew, nineteen, back then, was nice.

Spaghetti. That's what we ate at the tapas bar! And I had stomach-ache. Wind, from the stress of it all.

Silence. I've always hated that with strangers.

Conversation, if both parties try and keep it going, can make a lot of things bearable, even if you talk a little bit of rubbish (not that I do), but gosh, say something!

He definitely had red sauce over his mouth, because at that point I remember I spoke up. I pointed to his napkin. If he didn't say I had nice eyes, he must have felt it, because I caught him looking at them once, twice, when we finished. Then, when the waitress came to take away our plates, he nodded a yes and said, 'Bill'. He paid in that way my father used to when he'd take my mother and me out for dinner at the Lodge Inn Carvery down Rochester Street on our birthdays, back in the day when he had money and his other leg. He'd slap down the five-pound note from his pocket on a plate, then lean back and hand the saucer to the waitress. Follow her backside.

But you know, Mary and her brother, David, escaped in the end (the book). She went on to become a famous gymnast some years later and beat Kornikievna, the gold medal holder. David did his law, graduated, and sued his grandfather, blaming him for being the main perpetrator of their entrapment (*Good on yer, David*, I remember thinking), and he gave his mother two of the millions to hide away on a remote Thai island for the rest of her days (even though deep down he couldn't forgive her for leaving his blood father in the first place). But the two of them, brother, sister, couldn't live properly with other people after that (they tried). They even had a son together.

When I went back to work that day, after the lunch with the boy at the tapas restaurant, Frances, my boss, was waiting behind the counter for me, sorting a box of stamps. She had this twinkle in her eye, and with her chin tucked well into her chest, she said to me: 'Was it a *fruitful* date, then, Deborah?' Like that.

I thought about the Smith's aisle with that book in my hand, and the point where I realised someone was peering at me, intently. My stomach flipped a little, inside—dropped —like when someone jumps you from behind? Yet, to this day, I still can't quite pinpoint the significance of that date and why it enters my head so frequently, and especially why I'd said, 'Yes' so readily to that boy with the dandruff and the greasy hair and the crooked teeth that were yellow—who still works, as it happens, for Leylie's Insurance Brokers around the corner from the post office where I'm now manager, but if I work it out, I'll say.

Nowadays, of an evening, when I sit with Father, after feeding him his soup and his sleeping pills, as he sits in his chair, I read to him *proper* romances, you know the kind like where girl meets boy, and they live happily ever after? He doesn't seem to mind these kinds *too* much. And, occasionally, when he really wants it, I'll let him take my wrist—just for a *little* bit— and run his palms up and down the lengths of my arms. Sometimes he manages quite a pull, at first, but then … as soon as the pills start kicking in, I shoot back up to the toilet, lock myself in, and get stuck into real books. Right now, I'm reading *The Vampire Virgins of Vengeance* trilogy by Fatiiga. They're *really* good.

BECAUSE

It's an odd thing when he's near you. Your arms bump, as he jumps off the truck. Heartbeat. Sounds weird when you say it like that, but it's the only way you can describe it. He grabs the plastic bags by the roadside, and he turns. You keep yourself busy sorting, putting the cans he's passed to you here, the bottles there, the bags of wrapping paper, reaching—and all the while you're aware.
Then:
'Alright, then?' he says, a massive smile on his face. He puts his hands on his hips and he squints up at you with one eye from the sun. His breath comes out cold.
'Yeah, yeah. You?'
'I'm good,' he says.
'Good.'
He swings his arms about at the empty pavement around him.
'I reckon we'll be done around here by about eleven, what do you think?'
'Yes,' he says. 'Yeah, why not?'
He jumps back on the truck, and he signals round to the driver to go. Your arms bump again as you head on towards the parish's other end for your final round.

It's been like this with you and Ernie for three months since he joined your refuse company—him lifting, you, sorting; you bumping arms.

The truck turns another corner, and—

'Do you know what?' he says.

'What?' You can just about hear him with the cars whizzing and the cold wind.

'I reckon you and me, we're lucky.'

Your heart jumps, and you look down at the kid in the front seat of the car below: he's unbelted and he's got his tongue stuck out at you.

'Oh yeah?' you tell him. 'And why's that, then?'

'Because,' he says, '*Because*.'

The truck slows at the parish's end, and the town's Christmas tree comes into view. This time you jump off with him, and as you stride towards the row of bins together, you've got your head down, and you can't stop smiling.

STAINS

She was jealous of the way his wife had placed his pants
upon his pillow, the tea beside his keys unscathed. He
was jealous of the way the cars in front had halted—
waited till her bright blue dress had crossed the street—

   (*phones buzzing, ignoring …*)

Both joined each other again inside, regardless, for a
macchiato, after— where neither spoke, nor smoked this
time, not until the rain had ceased its beat.

OPPOSITE THE HILL JUST AFTER THATCHER'S '91

The house they attained was detached, but not double fronted. After they'd been there a year, no more, the construction of a porch, protruding slightly more than they'd originally envisioned, added the final sprinkle to their accolade.

You take your shoes off, leave them on the welcome rug, hang up your coat on one of the brass coat pegs, and you step in—

The hallway comprises of a navy-blue thick carpet, peach-slashed, which—when you open the double-fronted, white-panelled doors on the right into the living room—blends perfectly with the apricot striped wallpaper: *vertical* stripes, note, because they elongate. They lengthen an otherwise low popcorn ceiling and do not, in fact, detract from the navy wallpaper (again striped, but wider here) beneath the dado rail. (That, they added just before the front porch job).

For a narrow living room, they've created a fine space: a cream, gold-threaded Chesterfield two-seater fits snugly beneath the bay window, framed with swags and tails in— you've guessed it—peach, gold and blue layers. The rope ties (they couldn't get the exact shade to match) are a dull rust; more of a brown— but they look majestic, still, from a distance, hooked at just the right angle onto those brass holders, their long tassels dangling.

Guild mirror: and what a hit this is above the fireplace topped with a spotlessly white shelf. *How on earth did you manage to find such an unusual flowy design?* — people ask, as they sit opposite it, on the three-seater Chesterfield, this time—the Big Daddy—drinking from cappuccino cups and resting them on the mahogany table below. It isn't, alright, white, in line with the wood paneling all around, but it is *eclectic*, and that is what they prefer.

No TV? We'll get to that later. Right now, there's the *adjoining* room … Take your eyes from the gold miniature quartz clock on the mantelpiece (the only ornament), through more double doors (smaller here), to the *intended* dining room.

There *is* no table, but they've seen one with a marble top and high-backed chairs at Keay's Furniture Store in Greenwich, London. It's Egyptian, essentially, in design, and takes three months to make; this is the *only* thing holding them back, because the company agreed to add a few individualistic features, like rounded edges (he preferred the original: sharp, but she insisted).

So, the TV, yes, is in the garage, because, *Why misuse such an enormous space?*: dark and light magenta paint rebounding ... according to alternating walls and pillar positions. In one section, they've created a play area, with toys on low shelving (Montessori design) and a round red plastic table with miniature stools, allowing the children to explore their own freewriting. The original three-piece suite, just as you walk in— they may as well use it— they'd spruced up with matching magenta cushions. It's great there after work (if you have time); one can just plunge there (definitely at weekends—on Saturdays for sure; no after school club runs from prep school then, plus they operate their fitness/beauty/wellness business half day on Saturdays, not seven till eight, like weekdays; however Saturday timings, too, might have to lengthen, realistically, and soon ...), and there they sit and watch 'Through the Keyhole', the only television show they manage together once a week with the children; as a family.

The rest? Well, there'smore ... like the study, in a burgundy paisley: the settee, Marks and Spencer's (a sofa bed, although you'd never tell, looking at it), and the heavy mahogany desk with a leather button punched swivel chair facing the window, overlook fields (because you never know when a visitor might need to stay, and- maybe play a scratch card game or two from the drawers there, as the inhabitants do, often, before the others get up).

The master, with its four-poster bed in the centre, her cousin from London has already copied its exact design, *exactly*, with porcelain flowered spheres on each pillar. What he doesn't realise, however, this cousin, is that it's the *Victorian* antique carpet look, with floral drapes and valance, made to order, here, in Oxford, only, he'll never quite master— just like the children's rooms, where sheer curtained canopies hoisted above their beds, sport green cushions: yellow and peach ducks on for the boy, and blue edging and with white bows for the girl—*They're just like twins those two … and teddies everywhere!!* But the conservatories. Wow. With so much light in the larger one. And it is herewhere they will put all the kiddies when they arrive, their youngest turning five. She'll stay up all night making the clown face cake with royal icing and little matching cake squares around the outside— each with a letter from C h a r l o t t e on top.

The kiddies will have a disposable cake box each, pre-packed, with miniature burger shaped sandwiches: one bite— cucumber and carrot sticks, a mini fromage sweet frais, and a packet of Cheesy Cheddars. They'll be high on cake afterwards anyhow. And when they finish their food, sat in a circle on the newly laid black and white tiled floor, in that bright, spacious, and infinite conservatory where their pet cockatiel in its cage hanging dare sing, the clown will be ready to entertain the whole class afterwards, on the lawn outside. Then—the puppet show.

Relatives will sit in the 'good' living room, talking and fetching food from the kitchen bar (she'll stay up all night making that too: fried rice, Chicken A L'Orange, Swedish meatballs and a pasta salad. Black Forest gateaux and cheesecake, bought, for dessert).

'It's a shame you didn't take my spare dining room table,' her mother will say, watching her thirty-year-old daughter glide with a box of face paints into the back garden crowded with posh mothers. 'Practically new, I told you. *And* teak is still in fashion, as well.'

'That's all beneath her now,' her father will say. 'Because when ours were young, a Sunday roast was good enough, with their aunts and their cousins.'

A guest will arrive at the door, and her parents will continue their conversation from the living room:

'But, Johnny, how can they possibly afford …?'

'Perhaps their business is doing really well, Tina.'

'Yes, but all this? In a year? And how long do you think it will take them to pay it all back?'

'God knows, the way they're lending to the young these days. Only He can see where this is going.'

She'll open the porch door, and—

'Wow,' another mother will exclaim, peering over her head into the hall, her little Charlotte's laughter echoing as she storms towards them to receive her umpteenth gift. 'You've done *so* much to this place. I heard about it, honestly, but truly, it's outstanding!'

And she'll look beyond this guest's head and see the hill— the small green hill she'd spotted when they first drove down this cul-de-sac to view the house. It was directly opposite it— this house where she'd imagined her children would grow and play.

SISTER/BROTHER

Sister holds Brother's hand past shop to stables. Sister
follows Brother up ladder to shelf with hay. 'Sit here,'
says Brother. 'Watch this,' he's turning ...
Sister sees Brother take rope: he swings. He swings, he
swings, he swings.
'Aaron?'
Sister sits on hay and waits for Brother. Sister swings
legs, she flicks sharp hay: 'I can *see* you ...'
Sister spots light up high from window. Sister points,
squints, she counts, she sways: 'Aaron!!'
Sister lies down, she hums, she's warming. Sister shuts
eyes; she drifts, she stays.

Sister's shook rough, she's scooped, took downwards.
Sister blinks: red, on concrete, hay.

  Sister's carried out to cold of nighttime. Sister's mum's
screams; a light's blue blaze.

    Sister calls, 'Mama!' Mama's fading ... 'My babay!
My babay! My babay!'

PUMPKIN CURRY

It had only been six weeks since their youngest had gone to university and already she hated the way that he chewed.

She'd made pumpkin curry for dinner, a recipe she'd picked up from her neighbour, Lisa, at their weekly meeting that day.

'So, what do you think?'

He slopped the pumpkin around his mouth, and she could see, see the sticky strings of orange mixed with his saliva—thick, then runnier, forming and reforming, as he opened and closed with every chomp.

'It's al*right*,' he said, swallowing. Conversation never came easy to him.

Highgate Close had been their home for thirty years. The children grew up there, Nick and Sam. When her father had offered him a deposit on the house after they got married—a wedding gift—he'd refused, preferring to take on the 100% mortgage offered by his bank instead. He was a stubborn man, and, back then, she, aged twenty-three, had thought it a heroic act, him, thirty-one, wanting to take total control and look after her his own way.

'You don't have to eat *all* the sultanas,' she said, looking at the growing pile he'd shifted with his fork to the side of his plate.

'I don't usually eat sultanas,' he said, and of course she knew what he meant was: *So, why are you giving me sultanas when you know I hate them?* But he would never verbalise that; she knew that.

The house had changed somewhat over the years since they lived there, and they had now stopped working. First, when she became chief librarian at their local community centre, they'd put her pay rise in instalments towards a 'morning room' where he would sometimes go and read, or she would sew once Nick and Sam were in bed, or where Roger, their tomcat, mainly, would lay on her shawl all day.

Second, was the ripping out of carpets, replacing them with laminate flooring: spillages were easier to mop up, then, plus it gave the house an earthier and warmer feel. Then, it was the upstairs—all from the increases, year by year he'd received as ground controller at the airport—re-decorating mainly, and the loft conversion for his model crafting when Nick and Sam hit their teens.

'I was a bit heavy handed with the recipe Lisa gave me, I'm afraid,' she said to him. 'It said a cup, but I think it must have been too big!'

'A *mug*, perhaps, did she advise you?' he smirked at her.

35

The truth was … she liked Lisa. She was so much freer than her in every way. She'd travelled the world and taught underprivileged children in Mombasa. She joined a boyfriend on a marine biology project in Papua New Guinea and left her children—a three and a half and a six-year-old—with their father's mother in Loughborough. She'd climbed Nepal's Mount Annapurna, for goodness' sake. What was there not to like about Lisa?

'I know, I know what you're going to infer again about Lisa as a *friend* …' she said. 'We only have coffee on a Thursday.'

And to Forever 21 that morning, as it happened …

'Oh, Rachael, Rachael. You're really gonna love this one, Rachael. Seriously. It's *soooo* so sexy. I mean, like, *really* sexy.'

Curtain aside, and … whoosh! Lisa standing there, 200 pounds of her: arms out, legs loose, boobs squashed, cellulite blobbing, and the khaki glitter costume visibly holding her two belly rolls in.

'Be nice for a swim afterwards, don't you think? Or in case I fall in. Ha!'

This time it was white water rafting in Costa Rica, and that was the day Lisa advised her to make him the pumpkin sultana curry.

'Would you like some more, love?' she asked him.

'There's plenty in the pan.'

He crumbled the tower of rice from the top with his fork.

'Let me get you some.'

'Rachael!'

'What is it, love?'

'I don't know what you're playing at, but it's not funny.'

'What do you *mean*, Bob?'

'Oh …!' He pushed his plate towards the table's centre, stood and marched past her through the kitchen, pulling the garage door behind him.

Plates washed, kitchen worktops wiped, floor swept, peppermint tea in hand, she flicked on the fifth episode of Britain's Got Talent she'd recorded for herself earlier. She heard the garage door click, then a shuffling in the hallway: 'What are you doing?'

'Thought I might go out for a walk.'

'What, at *this* time?' She turned back to the screen, where a panel were critiquing a lithe twenty-year-old lad. 'The trouble with *you* is,' they began.

She blew in her cup, then put her feet up on the bean bag—a sweet spice smell in the air—when Roger, the cat, traversed her knees; she patted him: 'There, there,' then, 'Oh,' she said, quivering, as the draft reached her legs once more. 'Too cold, was it, again, for you?'

He placed his boots back on the rack inside the cupboard under the stairs and, still wearing his waterproof, went in and sat down beside her. He took her hand—Roger leapt down—then kissed her temple. She tilted her head to his shoulder as they watched the next contestant stride on the stage to sing.

AT AUNTIE LOL'S

When I was twelve, my mum sent me to stay at my Aunt
Lola's for a week in Shepherd's Bush. I'd never slept at
anyone else's house before, and all I could think of was
Madam Tussauds.

My aunt made me hoover the stairs, bake chilli cheese
scones for her shop, and shave my legs.

In the evenings, we ate cod roe on Ritz crackers by the
electric fire in her small living room above her shop, and
we watched The Tommy Cooper Hour show.

Sometimes, Terrence, from the Memorabilia shop next
door, stayed on upstairs to chat with Auntie Lol.

At night, because I wasn't allowed the light on, I'd wait
until the clock on the landing struck one and Aunt Lola
was in bed for an hour, and I'd creep past her bedroom to
the living room, to look outside. Down below, the
streetlamps shone, and there were no pub crawlers in
sight.

One nighttime, when I got up, and the clock on the
landing struck two, I crept past Aunt Lola's room, and as
I opened the living room door, I saw her, on the floor,
with Terrence, in a waxed embrace. Outside, and
opposite the street—rain fell in sherbet lemon drops.

The clock struck four and I got up again and went downstairs. Through the shop's glass window, Michael Jackson in a gold-black suit, leaning on a lamppost, his body half turned: a smile at me, and a wave, with his single, sequined glove.

Behind the counter, in the shop, Farah Fawcett handing a Battenberg cake to Elton John, and on the floor by my feet, my kitty, Pebbles, out cold from eating rat poison. Aunt Lola, on the final day, asked me if I remembered my things. She drove me back to Tulse Hill past Fulham—not Tussaud's—and said to give her love to my mum.

When I got in, an envelope, in my case, on the top, said: 'For you.'

I opened it, twirled, and slid on the sparkling, sequined glove.

HAMSTER

I bought my kid a hamster. He'd been going on about it
for ages. I'm really not an animal lover myself. Wait. Let
me re*phrase* that. I *like* them. Yorkshire terriers … their
faces, I 'spose. Cats, though? Uh-uh. I can't stand the
way they get all heavy and they sit on you, knead their fat
claws into you. Nah. And that dog stinkwhen the door
opens of people's houses who keep them inside? By God!
But they're ok. They're al*right.*

Anyway, hamsters …

I took Jack to a friend's house at The Meadows. Birthday
party. All the kids were there. His classmates.

'Look, Dad,' he said to me (twenty-six nine-year-olds
tearing about the place). I knew it was a decent school
and all, that's why I moved us here; not private nor
anything. But I'm telling you, some people around here
are making mega bucks.

'Dad?'

'Yes, Jack.'

'Rabbits, then …? For my birthday?'

'Is that a bowling alley there, Jack?'

'No, a cinema. The bowling alley's that way.'

'Whoa …'

'So, can I take one of these rabbits, please?'

'It's not yours, now, is it, Jack? Anyway, you know your granddad's got asthma.'

'I'll keep it in my room.'

'Jack, get in the car.'

He went on and on about it. Rabbits this, hamster that. When his birthday came, call me soft, I went to the pet shop. Dad was home, as usual, on the sofa.

'I went to the pet shop today.'

'Why?'

'A *rat!*' I shouted, testing him out. 'That won't bother you, will it?'

'I can't hear you. EastEnders is coming on.'

He sliced me sideways, that look … as I left with it in its carrier box.

Brown and white. *Fawn.* Easy to look after, the woman in the pet shop said. Alright, I said, that'll do. Just keep him busy, she said.

So I got him a wheel. Sharp little face. Puckered-up ears. A bit sly, though …

I put him on the kitchen worktop where Jack goes straight to when he comes home from school to dollop crackers with jam.

'Woooaaahhh, Dada!' he said, and he hugged me some. I tell you that felt *good.*

'Alright,' I said, 'Alright. There's a book there. Shows you how to look after it for real. Now go, take it to your room. Go on.'

Dad started sneezing, but I had no time, no time, what with Christine coming at the weekend and all. I had to think.

Hoover. Do that first—

I started, and Dad batted me with a newspaper as I worked around his feet …

'Bloody beggar,' I said. 'Just lift 'em, will ya?'

He never does nothing. Just sits. At least I got myself a job, building my business, bringing up my kid right, and letting *him* stay here! What's *he* ever been good for?

'You got me my tablets, yet?' he said, scratching his nut.

'Alright, then. I'll go for my walk, then.'

'Yeah,' I said. 'And say hi to your betting shop mates while you're at it, will ya?'

'Shut your face.'

Monday. Party's Saturday.

But I still got thinking. Balloons. That's what *she* would do, isn't it? Fancy cakes and all sorts of bits, probably. Nah. Hotdogs! That's what ten-year-old lads like. And PC games. I got him the Star Wars Force Awakens Pack. They're gonna love that.

Two days on and Jack had the rat running up and down his arm. He said, even though it was a 'white dwarf winter variety' hamster, you can get them quite friendly.

'He's not white, though,' I said.

'They don't always have to be,' Jack said. 'He's a *hybrid.*'

'Oh,' I said.

'Read the book,' Dad said.

'*You* read the book, then? *You* read it?'

'Actually, I have,' and he caught little Harry with his hand over from Jack's, letting him run all the way up his arm, across the back of his shoulders and down the other arm. He was chuckling! They both were!

'Come on you little fella,' Jack said, cupping him in his hands.'Time for dinner.' And he dropped him in the opening at the top of the cage, tapped down the latch.

Next morning, Jack was on a trip to the Isle of Wight with his school. I was to pick him up Saturday, morning of his party. He made me promise to look after Harry well. Waved at me from the bus.

So, I kept him on the worktop in the kitchen on all those newspapers.

But come Friday, I got home late from the brickworks … all those shopping bags … and Harry had gone berserk-like, running up and down in his cage like some madman.

He was swinging from the bars up top, chewing, gnawing at them.

'Well don't look at me,' I said. 'They're both out, I told ya.'

I tried to fit the Iceland chips packs, the choc-ices into the freezer, but he wouldn't stop squeaking. He was driving me barmy!

'Come here, you little stink,' I said. 'I got stuff to do.'

And I put him on the floor by the patio doors near the toilet. He was hissing at me!

I went upstairs and looked in Jack's hamster book.

Things which may cause your hamster stress:
Do not handle your hamster for 2 days after bringing it home.

Fat chance. At least from my side, anyway—

Keep your hamster in a quiet place away from noise. Noise will cause your hamster stress.

Did he think this was The Savoy?

Your hamster should not be placed on a windowsill, or under direct sunlight.
'Oh.'

Dad walked in, hanged his cap on the banister: 'Did you miss me?'

'What's in the bags?' I said. 'You had some good winnings, have you, whilst you've been away?'

He went back outside. Clanked about in the shed, by the sounds of it. Left me at the top of the stairs, yelling: 'Oi!'

He came back in, straight to the kitchen. Made loud scrunching noises.

'Shhhhh!' I said. 'You'll stress him out.'

'Who?'

'Henry.'

'You mean, Harry.'

'Yeah, him.'

'Oh, he'll be *alright*,' he said, snapping open a beer can.

'Oh, "he'll be alright", will he? Says he, who's not even had one look in since Jack went, let alone clean out its cage. Thanks for the offer, though.' I grabbed myself a beer can.

'It's me *asthma*,' he coughed.

'Yeah, yeah …'

'Where is he, anyway?'

'At the back. Dining room. Floor.' I took a swig.

'No, he's not.'

'What do you mean, he's not?'

'In his cage.'

'Where …?'

And we both knelt over it.

Sure enough, Harry was nowhere to be seen. He wasn't in his house, he wasn't under his bedding; we checked—nothing.

'He's escaped,' Dad said.

'Thank you.'

'You must have left a window open.'

'I did not. Maybe you did.'

'You're always opening them windows. Bloody clean freak.'

I shook the cage about a bit.

'Small enough to squeeze through them bars, I reckon,' slurped his beer. 'Ha ha.'

'What you laughing at?'

'Can't even look after a hamster.'

'Don't you need a nap about now or something?'

'Alright, alright … keep your breeches on,' and he started coughing that stupid cough of his.

'You never were good with them animals, though, were ya? Back when you were Jack's age.'

'That's 'cause you left me to look after them all day! Never once came back when you said you would. You and your bloody drinking.'

'Yeah.' Slurp.

'Stop making those noises.'

Burp.

'Nice.'

'You ought to get her to visit more, you know, Christine. Weekdays and all. Wish I'd done that, reached out, after your mother left.'

'I can look after my own affairs, thank you.'

'A lad needs his mum, is all I'm saying.'

'Yeah, well things are different between us now.'

'*Compromise* is women. *Understanding* …'

We both looked through the patio doors at the overgrown grass outside, and I pictured Mum, then, putting me to bed, her angelic face … then Christine, with her other half …

'Course, you could always get him another one before he gets back. Iwould. A male, same sort.'

'Have you finished??'

He got up, coughed some more, built it up well, and grabbed his beer pack.

'I'll go and stay at Bertie's again, then, since I'm not wanted around here.'

'Yeah, you do that.' (*Just as you always did when Mum had to work late, nights*).

And so, I was left to look for Harry myself.

I searched behind the curtains; I looked behind the loo. I went under the kitchen cupboards, the armchairs, I moved the settee. What the …? Where *was* the little blighter? This was all I needed.

Saturday morning, and there was still no sign of Harry in the house. Nor Dad—surprise, surprise.

What did I do?

'Give me another one,' I said to the pet shop assistant. 'Same as before. Identical.'

She smiled a funny smile, and I came home with it.

An hour before Jack's coach arrived and the hot dogs were ready; his football cake was in the fridge, candles lying beside it.

The coach was an hour late. He didn't stop blabbing in the car about his holiday.

'There were donkey rides, Dad, glass blowing, a party … and this girl!'

'Oh, good, Son,' I said. 'Good, good. Glad you enjoyed it.'

'How's Harry?' he said.

'He's good. He's in your room.'

Then I told him everything. I told him about old Harry escaping, how I hunted for him for hours, a whole day. I told him about the new one. I spilled the lot.

He went quiet for ages, then he said: 'Did you look up the fireplace, Dad?'

We got home and Jack belted it up the stairs. He didn't even notice the banner in the hall with his name on, the blue balloons.

I went to the kitchen, started picking up plates, moved them around. I looked over the worktop: cough. His Lordship was back on the sofa, football-watching. He scanned me over.

'What?'

'I never said nothing,' he said. 'But something's rattled your cage.'

'Yeah—you.'

'Thanks for me tablets by the way.'

Then we heard tumbling coming down the stairs and Dad's ears pricked up.

'Woah, Dada!' Jack was breathing all heavy-like, wrapping his arms around me.

'You, you like him, then?' I said.

'I knew you were fibbing, Dad. I knew it. Thank you, though. Thanks, Grandad. Thanks, Dad! This is the best birthday ever!'

I looked over at Dad. Then I figured Jack saw the PC game on his bed, and I relaxed.

Dad got up, coughed … wheezed his way to the toilet, batted his newspaper against his thigh.

'Come and see, Dad!' Jack said.

So, I went up with him.

Up in Jack's room, and he told me, 'I thought I was only allowed one, Dad!'

'Oh, yeah?' I looked down under Jack's desk.

Two cages …Two bloody hamsters. One was on a wheel going berserk, the other was munching a big fat seed. What the …?

I picked up the birthday card on Jack's desk. A great fat bulldog's face on the front cover, and inside, a familiar scrawl: *To Jack.* Jack looked up at me. *It says in the book they live better as a couple, so I got him a wife. Happy birthday. Grandad. Kiss. Kiss.*

'Yes!' Jack said. 'Now we can breed them!'

I looked out Jack's window to see if Christine's Jeep had arrived. Downstairs, a door slammed.

Still, I thought, if push came to shove and Old Harry did turn up again, we could always give it to Christine's little girl, Theresa, and have a bloody rat party, the lot of us.

ACKNOWLEDGEMENT

I'd like to acknowledge Katia Coquillon for the beautiful illustration of this book.

Nitsa Anastasiades

—the author

ABOUT THE AUTHOR

Nitsa Anastasiades

Nitsa Anastasiades was raised in UK, London. She holds an MSc in Creative Writing Fiction from Edinburgh. Her work has appeared in Black Moon Literary : 'What Constitutes a Beautiful Book?' , NoiseMedium Literary, and recently her fiction and poetry were commended by the Bridport Prize and the Fish Publishing Prize.

Her second book - OUR FOREIGN BORDERS - a collection of stories set in cities around the world, concerning themes of loneliness, alienation, the sexes, landscape, culture, prejudice and displacement, issues influenced from her travels when working in 11 different countries teaching English, is out now.

Currently living in Noida, Delhi, Nitsa is working on her third book, a novel - Sea with Salty Water - an exploration into the Greek Cypriot diaspora post 1950's EOKA war, juxtaposed with her upbringing in 70's/80's Britain and the 1974 Cyprus coup.

PRAISE FOR AUTHOR

"This is an excellent collection with shifts between long and short form, depicting the divides in British society and the hypocrisy and pain that lurks just beneath the surface. It is really strong, very well written, whose endings echo long after the stories are finished." Iain Maloney, author of 'The Only Gaijin in the Village'.

"We are pleased to report 'That Date with the Boy at the Tapas Restaurant' (from this collection) was selected ... which puts you in the top 7% of entrants worldwide."

- THE BRIDPORT PRIZE FOR SHORT STORY FICTION, 2022

Printed in Great Britain
by Amazon

43520671R00037